P9-DCN-311

THERE & BACK AGAIN

HAROLD JONES

A Margaret K. McElderry Book
Atheneum · 1977 · New York

Copyright © 1977 by Harold Jones   All rights reserved
Library of Congress catalog card number 77-3474
ISBN 0-689-50095-5
Printed in Great Britain   First American Edition 1977

Bunby felt cross and lonely. Richard and Lucy had gone away for
the day and left him behind.

Suddenly
he had an idea.
He would go out for
the day in Richard's
sailing boat.

He went down to the
kitchen and made
himself some
sandwiches for his
lunch.

But when he was ready to set off he found that he could not carry
the boat to the stream on his own.

He asked the dog to help him but the dog was too lazy. Then the
Siamese cat came into the room.

She and Bunby carried the boat to the stream.

"Goodbye," said Bunby.

Soon he was sailing quickly down the stream past all kinds of
animals, who gazed at him in surprise.

It was the first time Bunby had been out alone. He felt very brave
and very excited.

But before long a great gust of wind blew the boat into the reeds.

Bunby was thrown into the water. And he couldn't swim!

He might have drowned. Two swans pulled him out just in time.

They couldn't save his sandwiches, however.

Bunby thanked them from the bottom of his heart and
they swam away. But how was he going to get home? The
boat was stuck in the reeds.

Bunby took off his wet clothes and hung them up to dry.
He lay down in the sun and soon fell asleep.

When he woke up sometime later, he was amazed to find a
pigeon standing in front of him. "What shall I do?" said Bunby,
"my boat is stuck in the reeds and I don't know the way home."
"Don't worry," said the pigeon, "you can fly home on my back.
But why don't you visit my friends in the forest first.
It isn't far away."

So away they flew, high above the countryside, over fields and farms.

The pigeon landed in a glade in the forest. Bunby was thirsty.

He leaned over and drank from a little stream.

When he looked up the forest

was full of animals!

They had all come to meet him. The squirrels brought him leaves

and berries to eat because he had lost his sandwiches.

And the owl entertained them

with a ghost story.

Then it was time to go.

Bunby came home just before Richard and Lucy. The cat and the dog were waiting anxiously for him by the door.

They both thought he had got lost.

And when Richard and Lucy returned, Bunby was sitting there as if he had never been away. The next day Mr Jones called round with Richard's boat.

He had found it in the stream a long way from their garden.
Richard and Lucy couldn't think how in the world the boat had
got there.
And Bunby never said a word.